P9-CJL-110

NO LONGER PROPERTY OF
SEATTLE PUBLIC LIBRARY

When Grandfather Flew

Patricia MacLachlan
Illustrated by Chris Sheban

NEAL PORTER BOOKS
HOLIDAY HOUSE / NEW YORK

For my children
and their families —P.M.

Neal Porter Books

Text copyright © 2021 by Patricia MacLachlan
Illustrations copyright © 2021 by Chris Sheban
All Rights Reserved
HOLIDAY HOUSE is registered in the U.S. Patent and Trademark Office.
Printed and bound in March 2021 at Toppan Leefung, DongGuan City, China.
The artwork for this book was made using watercolor, pastel, and graphite.
Book design by Jennifer Browne
www.holidayhouse.com
First Edition
1 3 5 7 9 10 8 6 4 2

Library of Congress Cataloging-in-Publication Data

Names: MacLachlan, Patricia, author. | Sheban, Chris, illustrator.
Title: When grandfather flew / by Patricia Maclachlan ; illustrated by Chris Sheban.
Description: First edition. | New York : Holiday House, [2021] | "A Neal Porter Book." | Audience: Ages 4 to 8. | Audience: Grades K–1.
Summary: As Emma grieves the loss of her grandfather, she reflects on their shared love of birdwatching.
Identifiers: LCCN 2020025780 | ISBN 9780823444892 (hardcover)
Subjects: CYAC: Grief—Fiction. | Grandfathers—Fiction. Bird watching—Fiction. | Birds—Fiction.
Classification: LCC PZ7.M2225 Whe 2021 | DDC [E]—dc23
LC record available at https://lccn.loc.gov/2020025780

ISBN 978-0-8234-4489-2 (hardcover)

My
grandfather
loved
birds.

When we were younger—
before his hair turned white
and when he could still see—
my older brother, Aidan, and I
called him "birdman."
He gave us binoculars so we
could be bird lovers too.

"Did Nana bird with you
before she died?" asked Aidan.

"No. She loved her field of horses. All her life she wrote love notes to her horses and hid them in the homes of woodpeckers, in the crooks of trees, in birdhouses all around. Maybe someday you'll find one."

"Nana wanted to be a horse in her next life," said Mother.

"What will you be?" I asked Grandfather.

"I'll let you know when the time comes," he said.

When our younger brother, Milo, was little,
he sat in his high chair playing with his
wooden blocks.
Milo saw what Grandfather saw.
And listened to what Grandfather said.
Milo was not a talker.

He said only what he needed to say:

“Water please, thank you.” “Night night.” “No.”

Milo was a listener. He heard how
Grandfather loved the look of birds,
their beaks and wings.

"I love their songs
and the way they fly.
The brisk wingbeat of
the sharp-shinned hawk,

the hovering kestrel,

and my favorite bird of all,

the high-soaring

bald eagle."

"Look up," he'd say to Milo.
"The eagle sees the full sky,
he sees the world!
And he sees you!! I want his eyes."

Milo saw the open sky,
the hills beyond
the faraway river, like glass in winter,
and the birds.

One day a chickadee flew into the
window and Grandfather brought
him inside.
He put the bird in a paper bag to
keep him still.

"His heart is beating! If he flutters
in the bag, we can help him fly again."

We were quiet, waiting.
Milo stared at the bag.

After a while, Milo began clapping his hands furiously.

“Bird!” he said loudly.

The bird was fluttering!
Grandfather took him out of the bag and placed him in my hands.

“Here, Emma. Hold him carefully.”

I could feel the beating of his small heart.
I went outside and opened my hands.

The bird sat there for a moment.
I could feel his little feet.

And then he flew.
And I cried.

Grandfather patted me.
“Amazing, isn’t it?” was all he said.

Grandfather said "amazing" another time.
One day Grandfather's eyes couldn't see
a bird he heard rustling.

"What's that bird? I hear him in the fruit
trees, but I can't see him."

Milo, standing by the window, put his
sippy cup down on the kitchen table.

"Cedar waxwing," he said,
looking up at Grandfather.

"Amazing," whispered Grandfather.
And then it was his turn to cry.

Later, my grandfather's favorite nurse,
Leah, came every day to give him the pills
he could no longer see, and to keep him company
when Mother and Father went to work.
A bed was set up for Grandfather in the
music room near the windows that
look over the bird feeders.
Sometimes Leah described the birds to
Grandfather.

"Blue above and bright rust below," said
Leah, looking through binoculars.

"Eastern bluebird!" said Grandfather.

"Beautiful!" said Leah. "I love this job!"

"I love it too," said Grandfather, making
her laugh.

Leah brought the fur she brushed from
her dog to put out in a small pot.
We watched the birds carry it off, and later
found the black and white bits in their nests.

"I hear juncos," Grandfather said.

"I call them snowbirds," said Leah, and
Grandfather reached across the bed to
take her hand.

And then, one day, when we all came home from school, Grandfather wasn't there. Mother and Father and Leah took us in their arms.

"But where is Grandfather?!" asked Milo.

And suddenly Milo ran outside, calling to all of us.

“There! Look up!” he cried.

A large bald eagle, soared high against
the cloudless sky.
After a moment, it slowly circled down
close to us—
so close we saw the surprising flash of his eyes.

“Grandfather got his wish!!” called Milo.
“He sees the sky.
He sees the world.
He sees us!
Grandfather flies!”

Milo stood for a long time, looking up higher and
higher and higher into the sky—
as always
not talking,
listening for the eagle's faraway call.

junco
sharp shinned hawk
eastern bluebird
chickadee